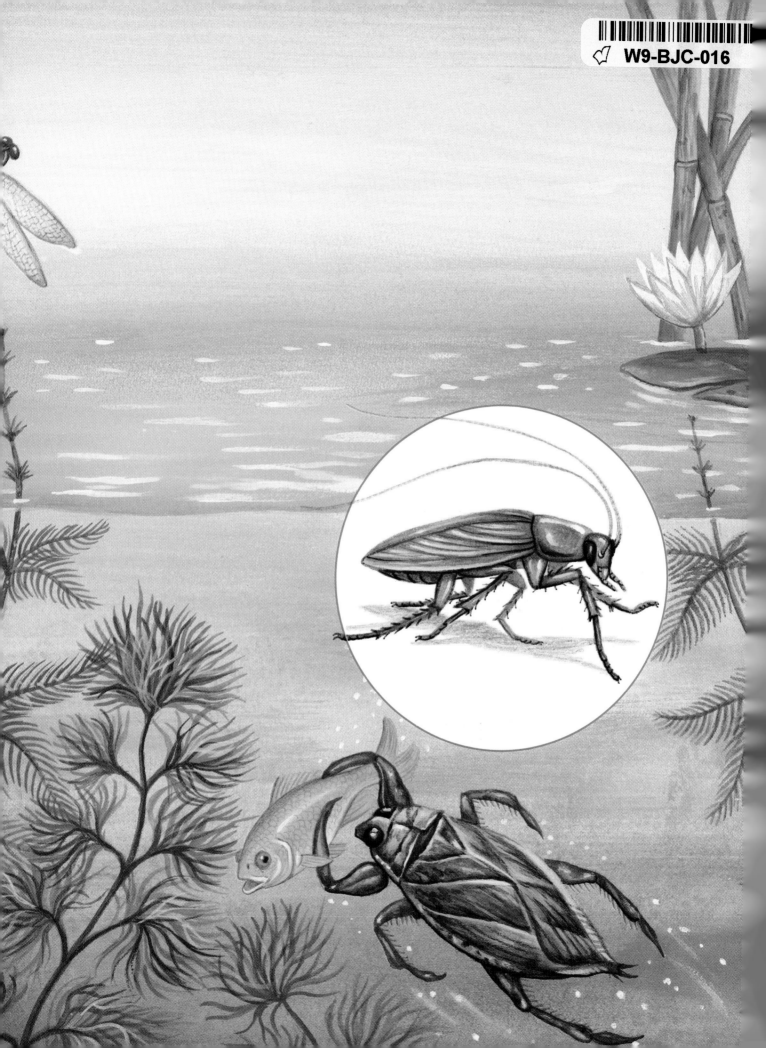

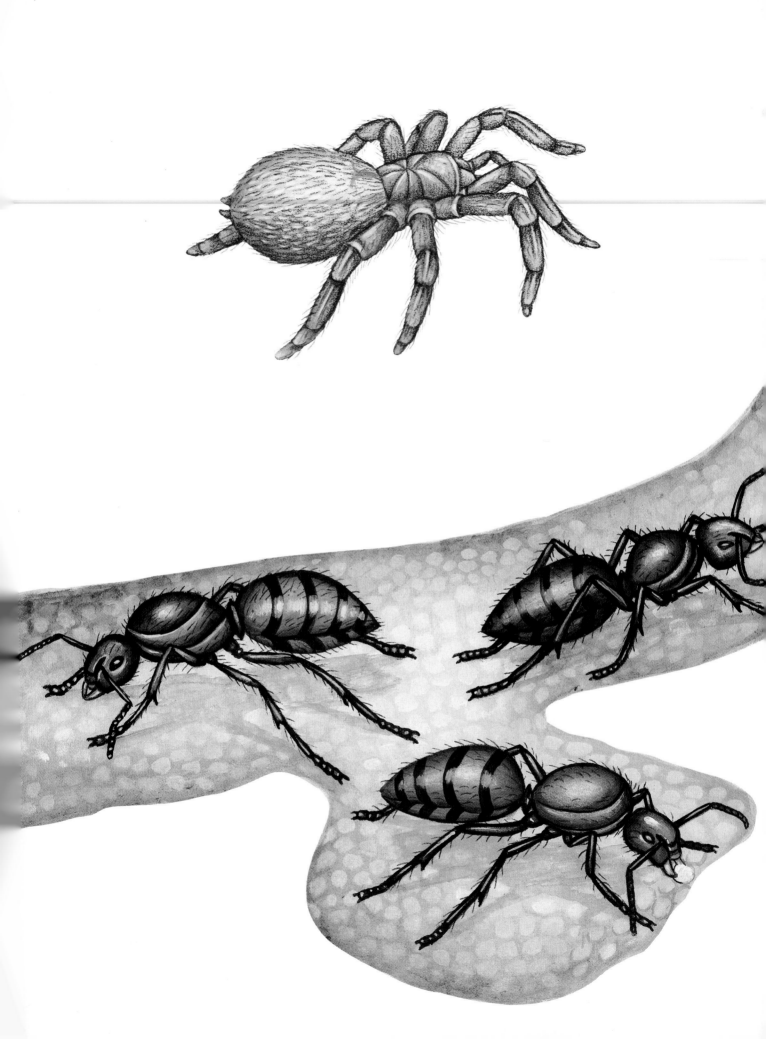

The Golden Book of Insects and Spiders

By Laurence Pringle
Illustrated by James Spence

Dr. Norman I. Platnick, Chairman and Curator, Department of Entomology, Museum of Natural History, Consultant

A GOLDEN BOOK • NEW YORK
Western Publishing Company, Inc., Racine, Wisconsin 53404

hummingbird moth larva

honeybee

Insects and Spiders

They are all around us—jumping, flying, running, crawling. Insects and spiders live almost everywhere on land, and some insects can also be found in fresh water. Most are small and easily overlooked, but they affect our lives in many ways.

Some insects spread diseases. Others damage or destroy food crops. However, these pests are only a small fraction of all insects. If some insects rank among our worst enemies, then others must be considered our best friends. We have an abundance of apples, grapes, other fruits, and many vegetables because bees and other insects carry powdery pollen from one flower to another. Plants need pollen to make seeds.

lubber grasshopper

garden spider

bumblebee

ladybug

Even more important, insects and spiders are part of the food webs of nature. They are vital food for songbirds, fish, and other wild animals. Many insects and spiders eat other insects and spiders and thereby help keep the total number in check.

We often take these small creatures for granted. By observing them and beginning to learn about their lives, we can discover that insects and spiders are fascinating creatures of great value, beauty, and mystery.

A World of Insects

Insects are a highly successful group of creatures. Their size enables them to live in such small places as the "jungle" of grass leaves in a lawn. Insects called fleas live in another "jungle"—the fur or hair on a mammal's body.

Nearly one million kinds of insects have been identified. Scientists believe that several million others may yet be discovered. Many may never be known because they die out when tropical rain forests are destroyed.

Insects cannot live in the salt water of the oceans, but they exist almost everywhere on land and are also found in fresh water. About 40 kinds of insects survive on cold, bleak Antarctica. Others live on the slopes of Mount Everest, 20,000 feet above sea level.

Mostly, however, insects live all around us. For every showy butterfly or flashing firefly we see, there are hundreds of other insects that go unnoticed in lawns, gardens, fields, and forests.

moths and butterflies

bees

beetles

flies

cicadas

dragonflies

bugs

grasshoppers

termites

earwigs

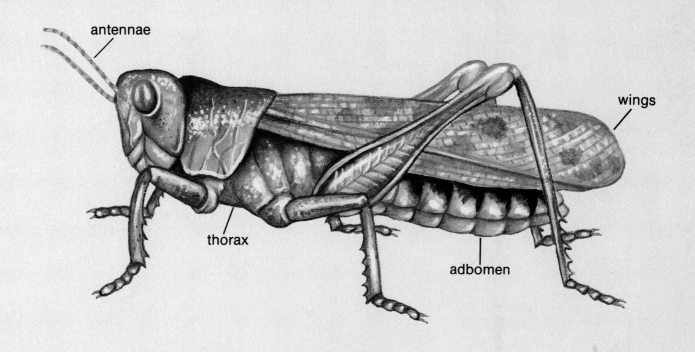

antennae

wings

thorax

adbomen

An Insect's Body

Insects come in many shapes and sizes. Some beetles are small enough to crawl through the eye of a needle, while large moths have wingspans of several inches. Nevertheless, the bodies of all adult insects have some features that set them apart from spiders and other small animals.

An adult insect's body has three parts: head, thorax, and abdomen. Above the eyes is a pair of antennae, or "feelers," with which an insect senses its world by touch or smell. An insect's mouthparts may be adapted to chew, suck, lap up a meal, or first pierce and then suck the food (female mosquitoes do this on your skin).

The thorax is an insect's locomotion center, packed with muscles that operate six legs. Many insects also have one or two pairs of wings on their thorax.

The abdomen is the largest part of an adult insect's body. Food is digested there. An insect also breathes through its abdomen, taking in air through tiny holes called spiracles. A network of microscopic tubes carries air all through an insect's body.

Insects also hear in interesting ways. Many of them hear either through the hairs on their bodies or by means of simple "eardrums" on their legs or sides.

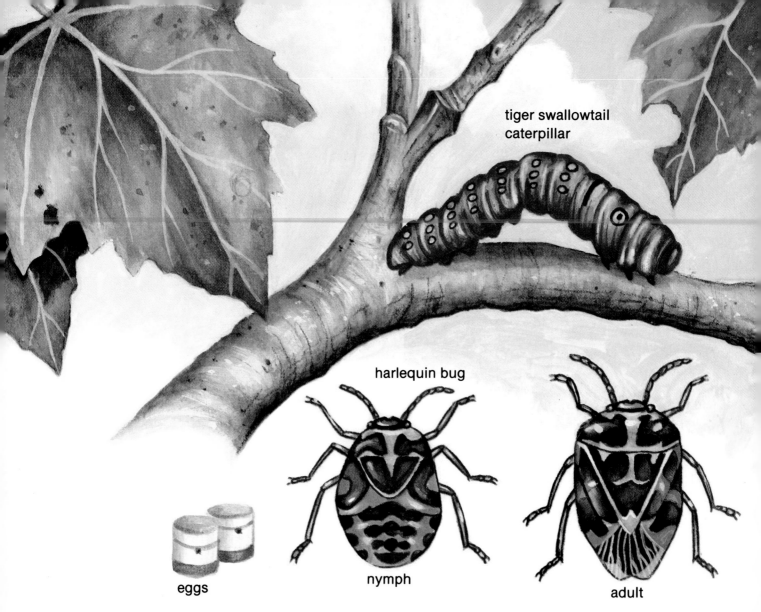

tiger swallowtail
caterpillar

harlequin bug

eggs

nymph

adult

How Insects Grow

Every insect begins as an egg, but different kinds of insects grow up in different ways. Silverfish and springtails were among the first kinds of insects on Earth. They still have a very simple way of growing up. When silverfish and other primitive insects hatch from eggs, they look like miniature adults. As they grow they molt several times. Their old "skin" splits open, and they wriggle out of it wearing a new, roomier skin. Silverfish grow in size but look the same throughout their lives.

Most insects pass through three or four stages as they grow up. Bugs and grasshoppers, for example, go through three stages: egg, nymph, and adult. When a bug or grasshopper hatches, it does not have wings. Each time it molts, the wings on the thorax of its new skin develop a little more. After the last molt, when the nymph becomes an adult, the wings are ready for flight.

10

butterfly emerging
from cocoon

tiger swallowtail
butterfly

Flies, moths, and beetles are insects that develop in four
stages: egg, larva, pupa, and adult. The larvae that hatch from
eggs are quite different from adults. Often they live in
different places and lead different lives. Fly larvae are called
maggots. Beetle larvae are grubs. Best known are the larvae of
moths and butterflies: caterpillars. (The name "caterpillar"
means "hairy cat," and many caterpillars are hairy.)

These insects go into a resting stage before becoming
adults. To begin this stage, many caterpillars spin a cocoon
around themselves. A silk moth caterpillar spins out a
thousand yards of silk thread while making its cocoon. Within
their cocoons or other "pupal shelters," insects go through
extraordinary changes. They enter as maggots, grubs, or
caterpillars. They come out as adult winged insects.

11

Bees and Wasps

The names "bee" and "wasp" make some people think of painful stings. Many bees and wasps do have stingers at the tip of their abdomens, but usually people are not stung unless they accidentally disturb a nest. One variety of honeybee from Africa is very quick to defend its nest and chase intruders. These African bees, sometimes called "killer bees," now live in much of Latin America and will reach Texas in the early 1990's. People have to be especially careful to avoid upsetting these bees.

Honeybees nest in the wild but people have raised them in hives and kept them for honey and beeswax for many centuries. We have learned a lot about their lives. Scientists have observed, for example, that a female honeybee working in a honeybee colony may have one of a dozen or more jobs. These include guard, scout, cleaner, and special attendant to the queen bee. (The queen bee actually gives birth to all of the young in the colony.) Fanner bees beat their wings to push air through the hive. Undertaker bees carry out the bodies of the dead.

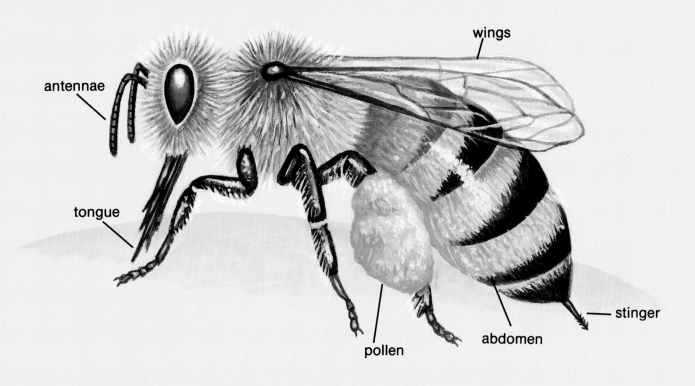

antennae

tongue

wings

stinger

abdomen

pollen

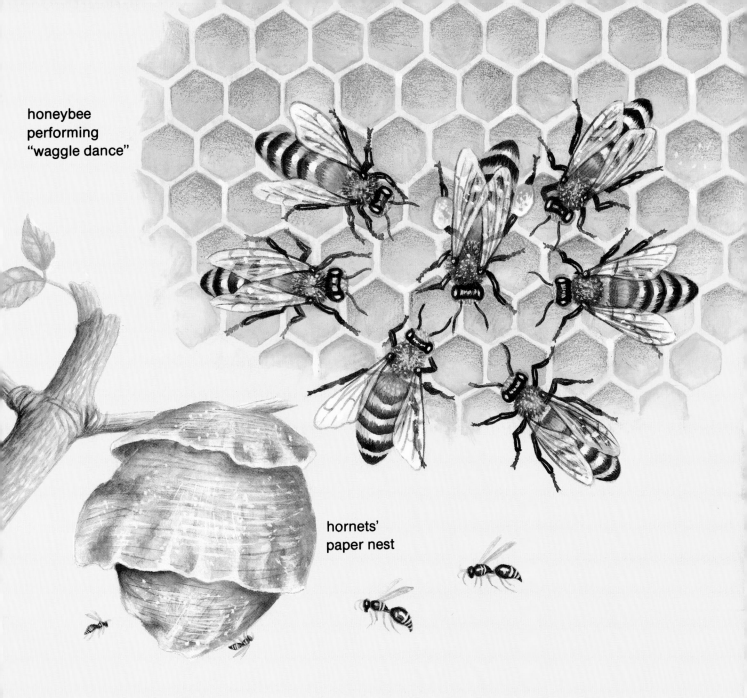

honeybee
performing
"waggle dance"

hornets'
paper nest

The toughest job is foraging for food. Forager bees may fly a mile or more in search of pollen or the sweet fluid in flowers called nectar. When they find some they make a direct "beeline" home and perform a "waggle dance" that tells other workers where to find the treasure.

The best-known bees and wasps are those that live together in colonies they build. Beside honeybees, these include hornets (a kind of wasp) that make gray-paper nests as big as basketballs.

Many other kinds of bees and wasps lead solitary lives. Many of them dig burrows in soil. Carpenter bees chisel tunnels in wood, and mud dauber wasps pack bits of mud into sturdy shelters for their young.

bat chasing diving
cottonwood dagger moth

Moths and Butterflies

More than 11,000 species of moths and butterflies live in
North America. In their caterpillar stage they are plant-eaters,
and include corn borers, cutworms, and other pests of food
plants. As adults, most moths and butterflies sip nectar from
flowers through a long tube that is kept coiled up when not
in use.

If you touch the wing of a moth or butterfly you will find a
sort of dust on your fingers. These are the tiny scales that give
the wings their colors. In a closeup view you will see that they
overlap like tiles on a roof, and look like the work of an artist.

Both moths and butterflies have antennae that are organs
of smell. Butterfly antennae are slender and end in a knob.
Moth antennae are usually feathery.

monarch butterflies

Some kinds of moths are able to hear the high-pitched sounds that bats use to locate prey. When a moth hears a moth-eating bat in the distance, it flies in the opposite direction. If a bat's calls are close, the moth folds its wings and dives for the ground. This special hearing ability helps moths escape capture.

Most moths and butterflies die in the frosty nights of autumn. In the following spring a new generation will hatch from eggs or emerge from cocoons. However, some kinds of moths and butterflies survive winter as adults. They seem lifeless as they hide under tree bark or in other sheltered places. A warm spring day brings them out. The mourning cloak is usually the first butterfly seen in the spring.

Monarch butterflies migrate from Canada and the northern United States to winter resting sites in southern California and central Mexico.

Different Ways to Catch a Meal

Some insects are predators, catching other insects for their food. The praying mantis usually stays still and ambushes its prey. (Watch a mantis turn its head. It is the only insect capable of looking over its shoulder.)

The ant lion, named for its fierce-looking larva, digs a funnel-shaped pit in sand or loose soil. The ant lion hides at the bottom, just beneath the surface, its jaws ready. It grabs ants and other insects that slip down into the pit.

Dragonflies spend the first three quarters of their lives underwater. As nymphs, they catch insects and other underwater life, including small tadpoles. As adults, they patrol the air near streams and ponds. They can hover in one place. They can even fly backward. Their bulging compound eyes contain as many as 28,000 tiny lenses. This gives them the sharpest vision of all insects. They catch mosquitoes and even speedy bumblebees on the wing.

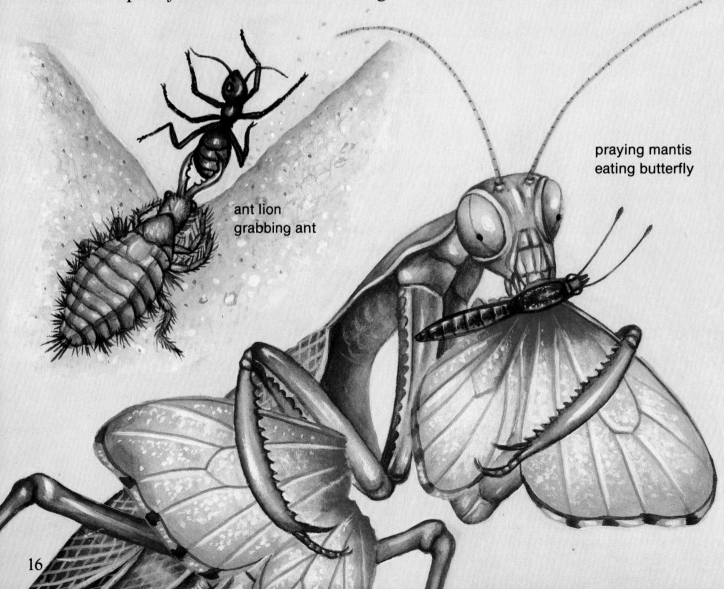

ant lion
grabbing ant

praying mantis
eating butterfly

16

walking
stick

treehopper

moth caterpillar

Hidden in Plain Sight

Many insects are masters of camouflage. Their colors, shapes, and behavior enable them to blend with tree bark, leaves, or other places where they rest. Some moth caterpillars resemble the twigs of trees they feed on, especially when they are resting on them.

Insects called walking sticks look like twigs, too. Treehoppers often look like little bumps or even thorns on the plant stems from which they suck juices.

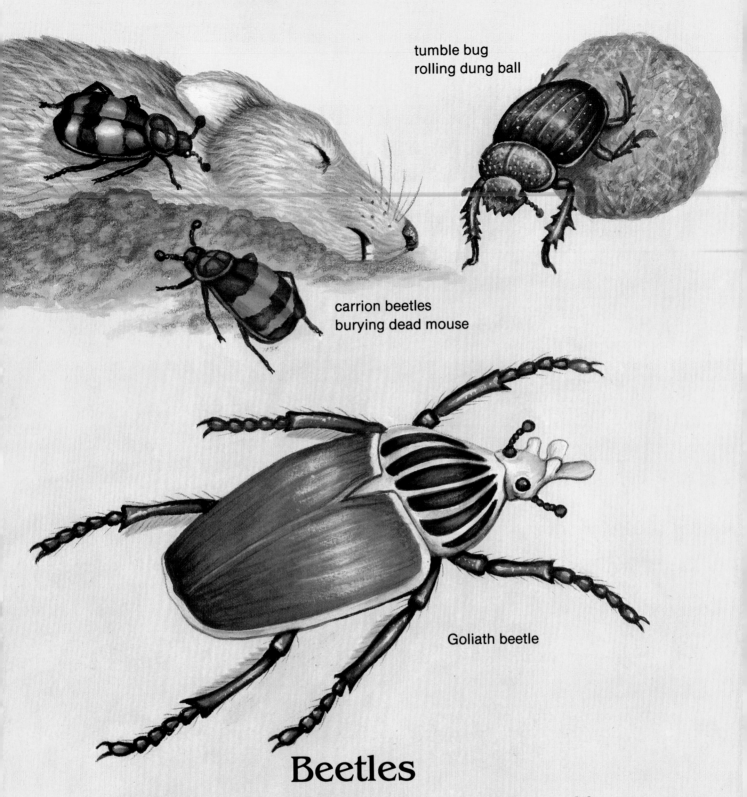

tumble bug
rolling dung ball

carrion beetles
burying dead mouse

Goliath beetle

Beetles

Of all animals on Earth identified so far, one out of four is a beetle. More than a quarter million have been named, and hundreds of new species are discovered each year.

This highly successful group is called Coleoptera, which means "sheath-winged." The front wings of beetles are hard shields that protect their rear wings and abdomens. This protection of their soft body parts enables beetles to burrow underground and squeeze under rocks without doing harm to themselves.

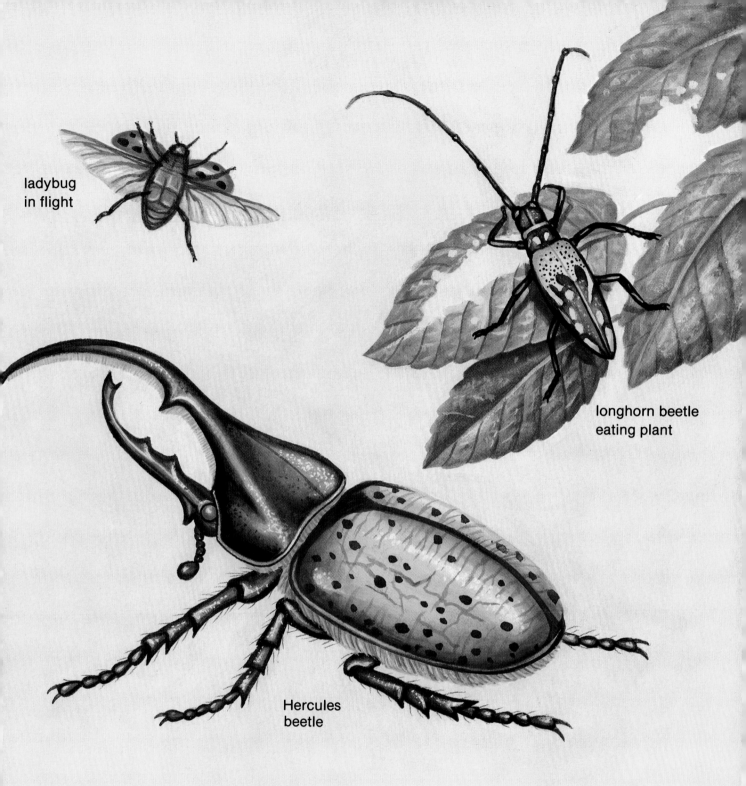

ladybug
in flight

longhorn beetle
eating plant

Hercules
beetle

Most beetles are plant-eaters. However, on land and in fresh water, beetles feed in just about every way imaginable. Some eat roots, others eat leaves, fruits, fungi, or even wood. Tiny beetle larvae called leaf miners chew a maze of tunnels in the narrow space between a leaf's upper and lower surface. Other beetles feast on dead animals and on dung.

Some common species of beetles have inaccurate names. On summer nights, fire*flies* flash their lights and June *bugs* hit against window screens. However, they too are beetles. So are weevils and ladybugs.

19

Ladybird beetles, as ladybugs are more accurately called, are predators. Both adult and larval ladybird beetles feed on aphids, tiny insects that suck fluids from plant stems.

Other beetles that are predators include tiger beetles, which have sharp vision and race over the ground to catch prey. Caterpillar hunter beetles climb trees in search of their favorite food—caterpillars.

Some large beetles—such as ox, rhinoceros, and stag beetles—have strong horns or pincerlike jaws. Despite the fierce appearance of these beetles, they are harmless. They use their horns or pincers in beetle battles. While fighting over food or mates, they try to toss opponents off plant stems with their horns or grab them with their pincers, and drop them to the ground below.

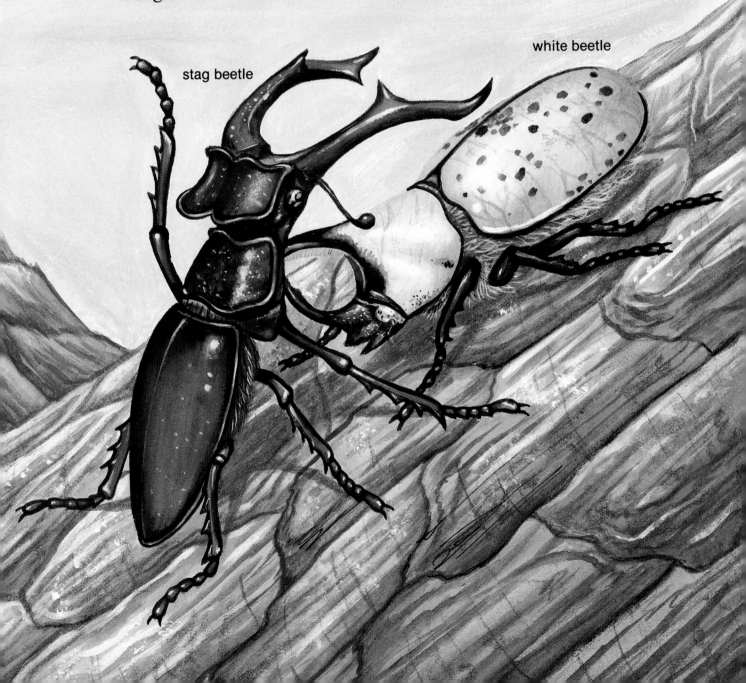

stag beetle

white beetle

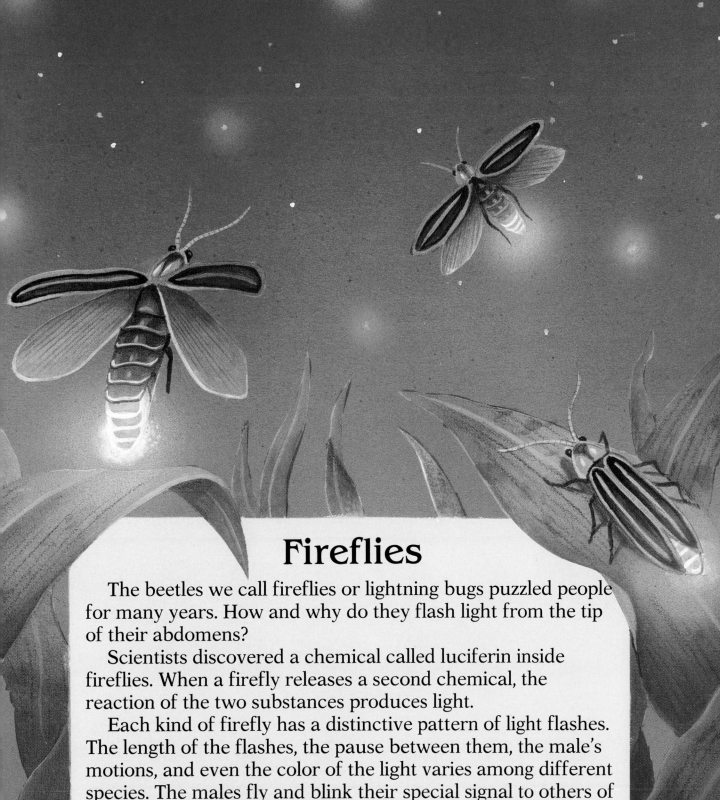

Fireflies

The beetles we call fireflies or lightning bugs puzzled people for many years. How and why do they flash light from the tip of their abdomens?

Scientists discovered a chemical called luciferin inside fireflies. When a firefly releases a second chemical, the reaction of the two substances produces light.

Each kind of firefly has a distinctive pattern of light flashes. The length of the flashes, the pause between them, the male's motions, and even the color of the light varies among different species. The males fly and blink their special signal to others of their kind. Females wait on plants or the ground and respond with an inviting flash. This is how they meet and mate. (In some species the eggs and larvae also glow a bit in the dark.)

Some female fireflies mimic the flashes of other species. They lure male fireflies in, then eat them.

Insects' Songs

Imagine you are camping out at night. You are comfortable in your tent and about to fall asleep. Then you hear one of the most annoying of all sounds on Earth—the whine of a female mosquito's wings. You may hate this noise but it is music to male mosquitoes. They detect the whine with their antennae and follow it in order to find a mate.

Many people like the sound of a field cricket's chirp. Male crickets make it by rubbing their wings together. Female crickets hear it through simple "eardrums" located on their forelegs. They follow the sound to find the male. More than 2,000 kinds of crickets have been discovered, and each species has its own distinctive song.

Summer fields buzz and hum with the songs of male short-horned grasshoppers. They rub their hind legs against their front wings to attract females. In the evening, tree-dwelling katydids make rasping sounds by rubbing together parts of their front wings. Over and over the males sing out "katy did, katy did"—the sound that gives the insects their name. Female katydids hear it through simple organs in their front legs.

Male cicadas make long, shrill hums by rapidly vibrating two drumlike membranes on their abdomens. When cicadas are abundant, their buzzing chorus fills hot summer days.

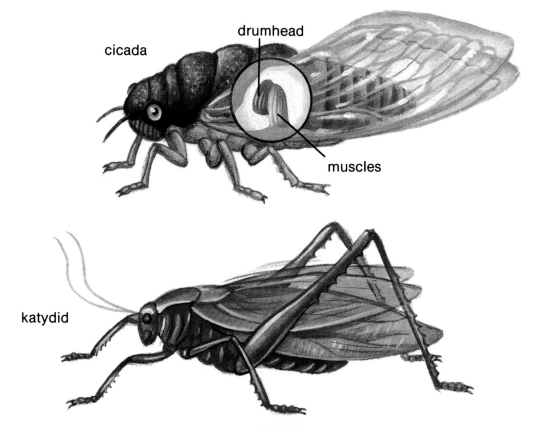

cicada

drumhead

muscles

katydid

blue jay

saturniid moth

Scaring Enemies Away

Yummy—an insect to eat! Many creatures, including bats, birds, lizards, spiders, and even other insects, hunt insects for food. While some insects flee, hide, or appear to be part of a plant, others are adapted to repel their enemies. Sometimes they scare them away.

Some moths and butterflies have large eye marks on their wings. These "eyes" are concealed when the insect rests but are displayed when it is attacked. Studies have shown that these marks startle birds and help the moths and butterflies escape.

When the larva of a tiger swallowtail butterfly first hatches, it resembles a bird dropping. After three molts, it is much bigger in size. It is now green and has two fierce-looking false eyes on its head. To a bird, the caterpillar may look like a scary snake.

Some insects mimic their predators. When a fruit fly called Zonosemata is stalked by a jumping spider, it spreads its wings and flaps them up and down. The wings have the same color pattern as a jumping spider's legs. Oftentimes these spiders wave their legs up and down to warn others of their kind to stay out of their territory. By looking and acting like a jumping spider, the fruit fly makes the real spider retreat.

23

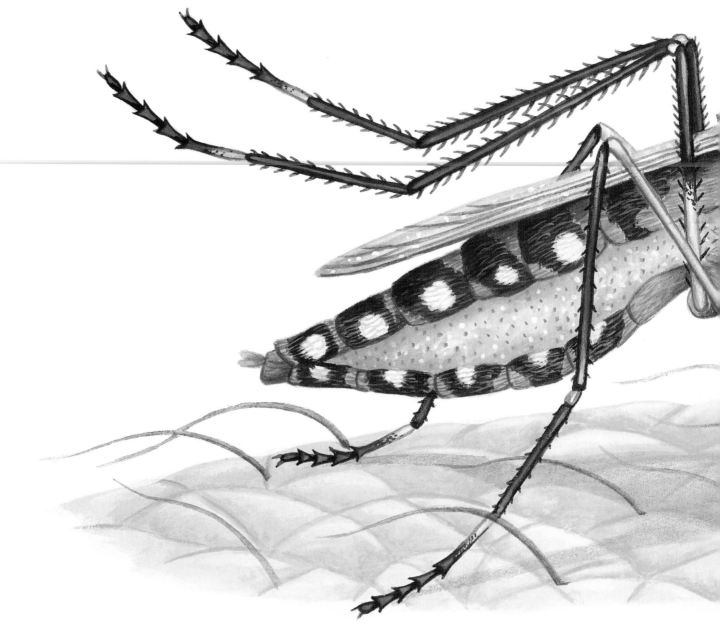

Flies and Mosquitoes

Flies are a large group of insects (called Diptera) with about 85,000 known species worldwide. Overall, most flies, like the crane fly, are harmless. Nevertheless, people swat many crane flies because these insects look like giant mosquitoes. Mosquitoes, along with deer flies, black flies, biting midges, and other Diptera members, are nuisances. One kind of midge is so tiny—less than a tenth of an inch long—that it is called a no-see-um. Swarms of night-flying no-see-ums are hard to see but when they bite you can still-feel-um.

Some flies and mosquitoes are much more than nuisances. They carry dangerous diseases, especially in the tropics. At least a million people die each year from malaria, carried by mosquitoes.

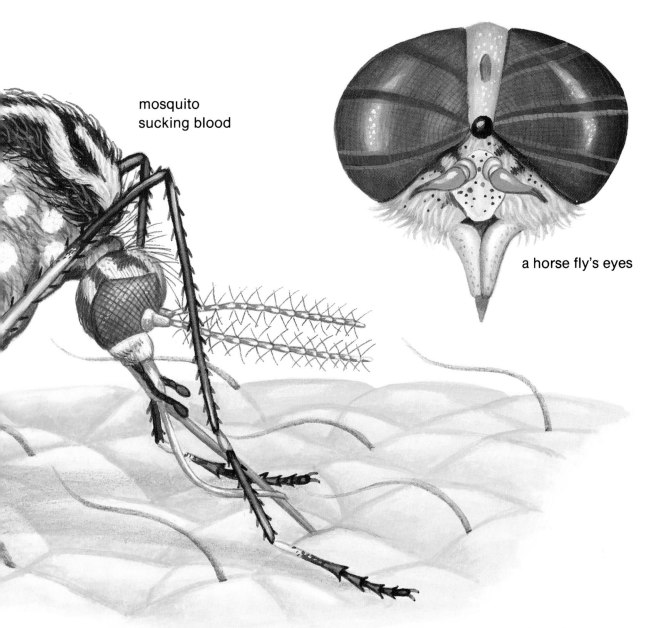

mosquito
sucking blood

a horse fly's eyes

Other harmful flies include fruit flies. Some species damage fruit by laying their eggs in the fruit. Their larvae feed and develop there. However, studies of fruit flies have added greatly to our knowledge of genetics—how traits are passed from one generation to the next.

Most flies suck sap or nectar from plants. But some take painful bites of flesh or pierce the skin in order to tap the blood they seek as food. Usually female flies do the biting and sucking. Like mosquitoes, they need nutritious blood in order to produce abundant eggs for a new generation.

The antennae of female mosquitoes are so sensitive that they can detect chemical odors and heat given off by a person's body. Frequent bathing removes some of the chemicals that lure mosquitoes. And people who eat garlicy foods or take B vitamins seem to repel mosquitoes.

Some Insects Are Bugs

Some people call all insects "bugs." In North America, about 3,800 species are truly bugs. All bugs have sucking mouthparts. Squash bugs, lace bugs, and stinkbugs suck sap from plants and are sometimes garden pests.

Most bugs live on land but some well-known kinds live in ponds, lakes, and streams. They include backswimmers and water boatmen, which have long back legs that row the bugs through the water.

Giant water bugs (up to 2½ inches long) also live in ponds. These true bugs are not found in bathrooms or kitchens of city homes. When people say they saw a water bug in such places, they have seen a large cockroach.

backswimmer

water
boatman

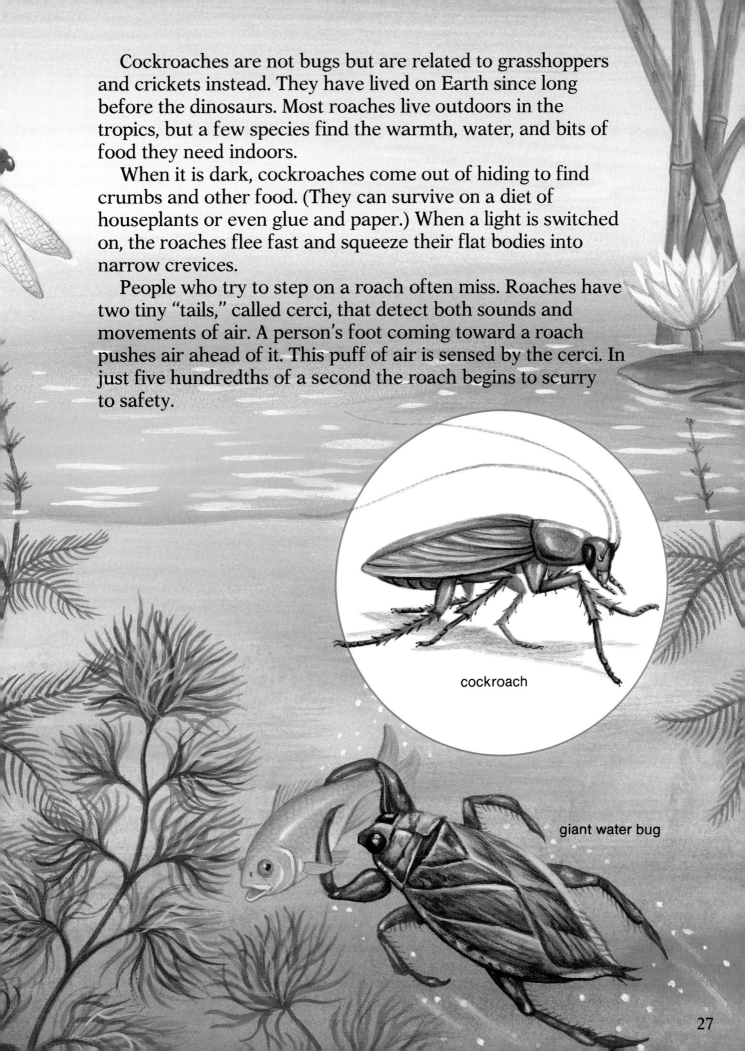

Cockroaches are not bugs but are related to grasshoppers and crickets instead. They have lived on Earth since long before the dinosaurs. Most roaches live outdoors in the tropics, but a few species find the warmth, water, and bits of food they need indoors.

When it is dark, cockroaches come out of hiding to find crumbs and other food. (They can survive on a diet of houseplants or even glue and paper.) When a light is switched on, the roaches flee fast and squeeze their flat bodies into narrow crevices.

People who try to step on a roach often miss. Roaches have two tiny "tails," called cerci, that detect both sounds and movements of air. A person's foot coming toward a roach pushes air ahead of it. This puff of air is sensed by the cerci. In just five hundredths of a second the roach begins to scurry to safety.

cockroach

giant water bug

27

Ants and Termites

Like honeybees, ants and termites are social insects. Each kind lives together in a colony that centers around one individual—a long-lived queen.

Even though at one point in their life cycles termites and ants look somewhat alike, as adults they are very different from one another. An ant has a distinct waist between its thorax and abdomen. Ants are usually dark-colored and roam about freely outdoors. A termite has no waist. Termites are usually white and avoid light. They spend most of their lives underground, inside wood, or inside tunnels and other structures they make.

Winged ants are good fliers but termites flutter weakly and soon land. Anyone who sees "flying ants" in or near their home should investigate. They might be termites from a colony that is slowly eating wooden parts of the house.

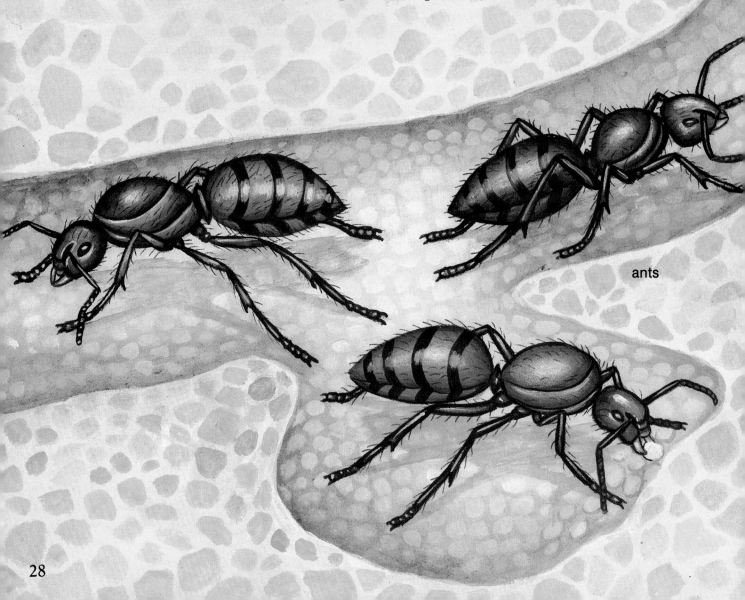

ants

28

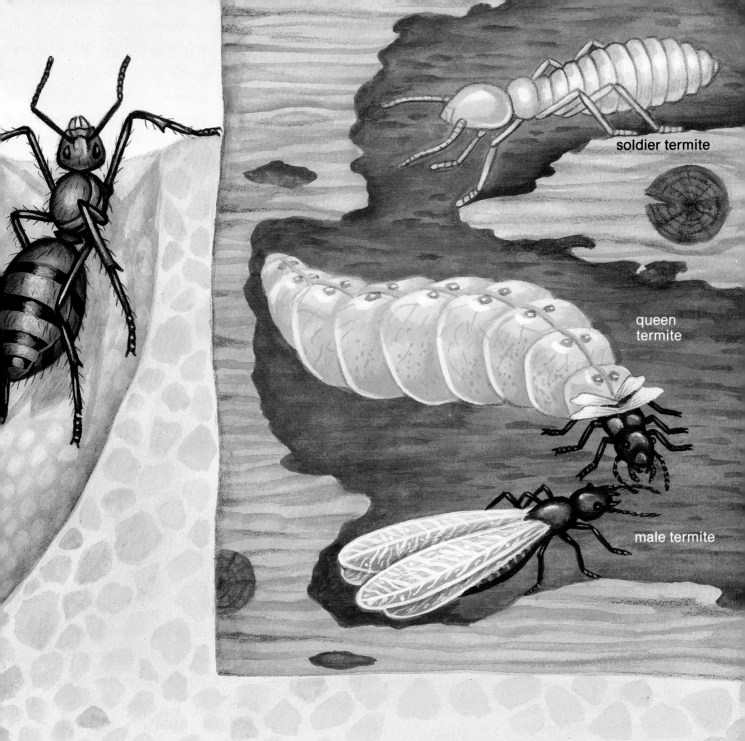

soldier termite

queen termite

male termite

Carpenter ants also live in wood but are unable to digest it. Most ants make their colonies underground. The site is often marked with a mound of earth that has been carried up, bit by bit, from a complex system of rooms and tunnels below.

From a colony of harvester or carpenter ants, lone foragers go in search of food. When they find some, they return to the nest, leaving scent trails that others from the colony can follow.

Some ants protect and care for aphids that suck sap from plants. The aphids produce a sticky, sweet fluid called honeydew that ants like. With their antennae, ants stroke the aphids, then lap up the drops of honeydew that flow from the abdomens of their "livestock."

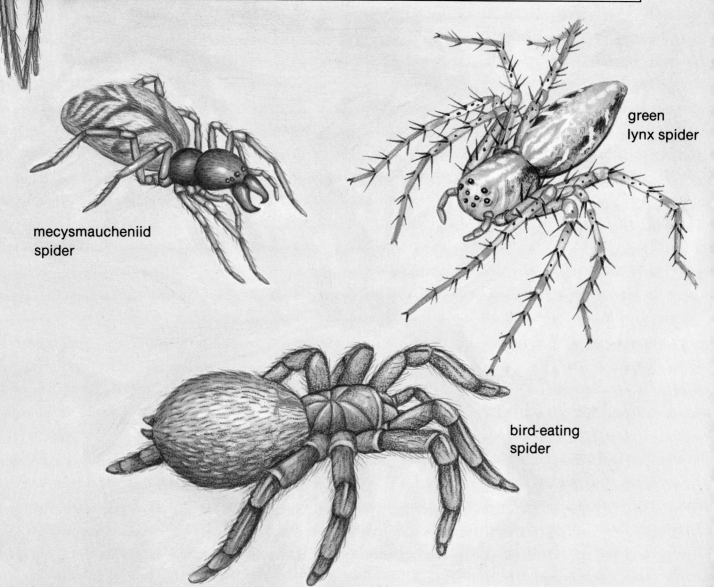

crab
spider

A World of Spiders

Like insects, spiders live almost everywhere on land. You may see them in lawns and gardens, and even in your home. All spiders are predators, killing insects and sometimes other spiders for food. In its lifetime a spider may catch hundreds of insects, including many that are pests to people.

Scientists have so far identified over 34,000 kinds of spiders. Since the spiders of many tropical areas have not been studied, scientists believe that 100,000 other kinds may be discovered.

Spiders are weavers, engineers, acrobats, and balloonists. They frighten some people but fascinate others. It can be fun to sit down beside one, watch patiently, and observe the happenings in its world.

cobweb
weaver

green
lynx spider

mecysmaucheniid
spider

bird-eating
spider

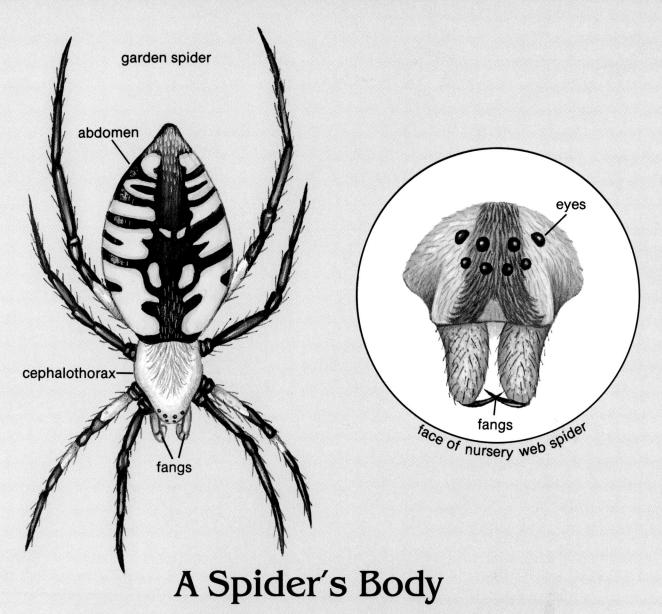

garden spider

abdomen

cephalothorax—

fangs

eyes

fangs

face of nursery web spider

A Spider's Body

Spiders have eight legs, two more than adult insects. While an insect's body is divided into three parts, a spider's body has just two main parts: its abdomen and its cephalothorax, a combination of head and thorax.

A closeup view of a spider's face can be startling. Most spiders have eight eyes. One pair may be bigger and gives sharper vision than the others. The smaller eyes are good at detecting motion anywhere around the spider.

A spider bites with its sharp jaws, tipped with fangs that inject poison into the body of an insect or other prey. This poison kills or paralyzes the prey. Then a spider injects chemicals that will turn the insides of the prey's body into a fluid. The spider sucks up this fluid food. Spiders have a liquid diet.

As spiders grow they must molt, wriggling out of their old "skin" like insects do. The "dead" spider you see on the ground or in a web may be just the cast-off skin of a spider that is still alive.

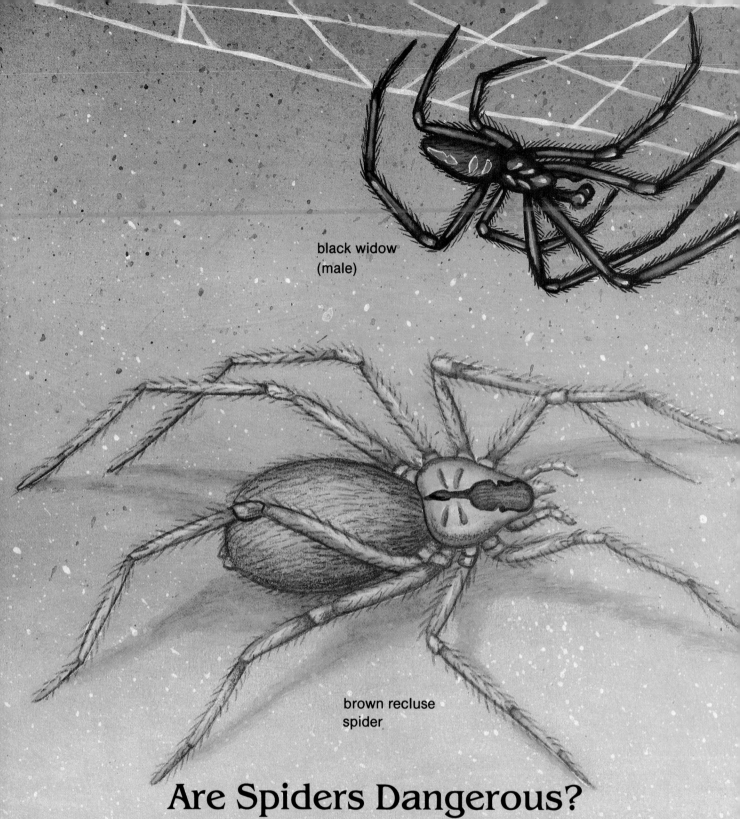

black widow
(male)

brown recluse
spider

Are Spiders Dangerous?

In the United States, death from a spider bite is extremely rare. Some people fear all spiders, but only a few kinds are dangerous. Their venom has no effect on people and a few spiders do not even have venom.

The bite of the brown recluse spider may leave a painful wound. This spider is sometimes found in homes. It has a violin-shaped mark on its cephalothorax, so it is sometimes called the violin or fiddleback spider.

black widow
(female)

Bites of widow spiders are more dangerous. The females of several species have fat, shiny black abdomens with red or yellow markings underneath. They are called "widow" spiders because they often kill their male partners after they mate. The male widow spider is harmless and even though the female rarely leaves her tangled cobweb home, people should avoid touching any spider with a glossy black body.

How Spiders Use Their Silk

All spiders have silk glands within their abdomens. At the tip of a spider's abdomen are tubes called spinnerets. Silk flowing from the spinnerets changes instantly from liquid to solid as soon as it hits the air. Spiders that make elaborate webs have five or more glands that produce different kinds of silk.

Most spiders do not spin webs, but they all rely on silk. One kind of silk is used to wrap the bodies of insects that will be eaten later. Another kind is laid down in a line behind a spider as it travels. This dragline enables a spider to drop safely from a height and to crawl back up later. The dragline also allows a spider to retrace its path to its home.

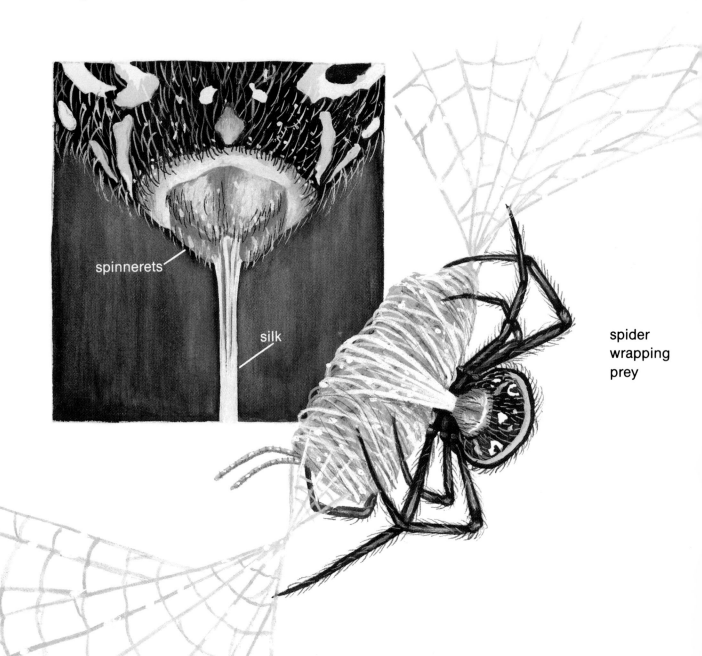

spinnerets

silk

spider wrapping prey

34

Some spiders make walls and doors of silk for their hideouts, and nearly all female spiders spin waterproof silk sacs for their eggs.

Silk also helps increase baby spiders' chances of survival. If spiderlings stayed close together after hatching they might all be eaten by a bird or other enemy. They would also hunt one another. It is best for the spiderlings to disperse. Soon after hatching, they climb to the tops of plants or other tall places. Then they let out lines of silk that catch the wind and lift them into the air. They go "ballooning." Spiderlings have been found sailing 14,000 feet above Earth, and 200 miles from shore. Most of them travel less far, and settle down in a new home on land.

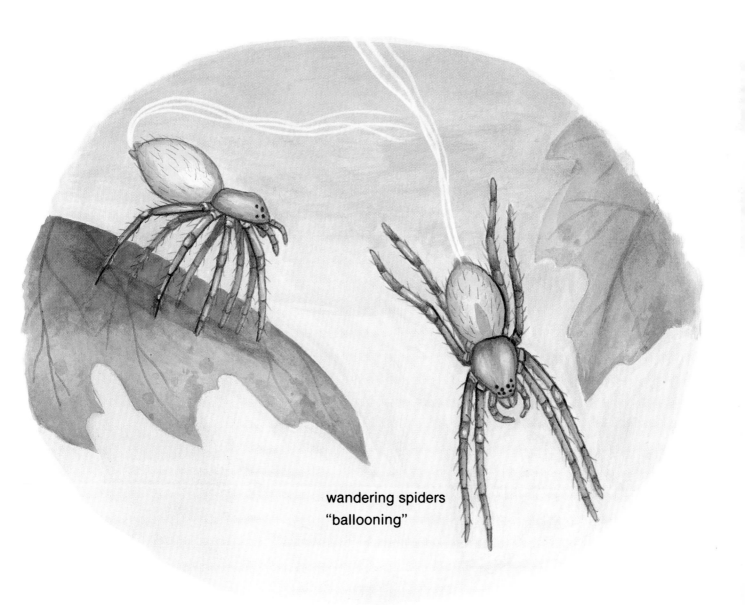

wandering spiders
"ballooning"

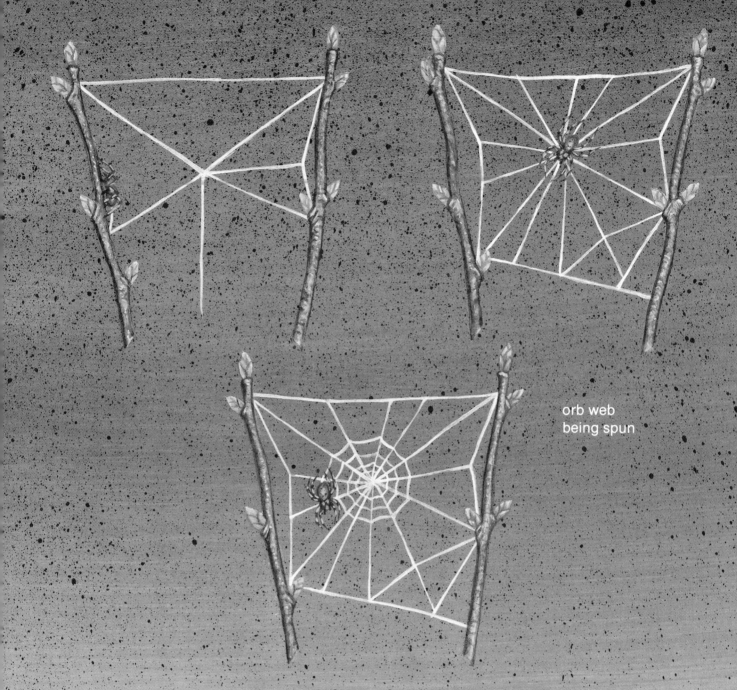

orb web
being spun

Web-Spinning Spiders

Web-spinning spiders cannot see well. They rely on their webs to catch food. Some spiders make webs that look like careless tangles. Others spin webs shaped like funnels, domes, hammocks, or wagon wheels.

In a wheel-shaped, or orb, web, some spiders lay down spirals of sticky silk. Others make spiral lines that are fuzzy. Either way, the spiral lines entangle insects that touch them. The spider waits for an insect to fly or jump into the capture threads. It feels vibrations in the lines as the insect struggles. The spider then runs from its resting place, gives the prey a poisonous bite, and soon has a meal.

People have wondered why spiders are not caught in their own webs. Spiders usually avoid stepping on their capture threads. Even if they do, however, they are protected from getting stuck in some unknown way. This is just one of many mysteries about the lives of spiders.

You have to get up very early or stay up late in order to watch an orb-weaver make its web. Some species build webs near or at dawn. They trap day-flying insects. Other species spin their webs in the evening, preparing for moths and other night-flying prey.

A spider usually begins to build a new web by eating most of the threads of its old web. Then it needs an hour or less to spin the intricate design of a new food trap.

Wolf, Crab, and Jumping Spiders

Many spiders are keen-eyed predators that ambush their prey, leap on it, or chase after it. Their names suggest their hunting way of life—there are wolf, lynx, crab, and jumping spiders. There are even fisher spiders that catch minnows and other small fish.

Wolf spiders have long legs and run swiftly over the ground after insects. Some of them hide in burrows that they dig with their strong jaws.

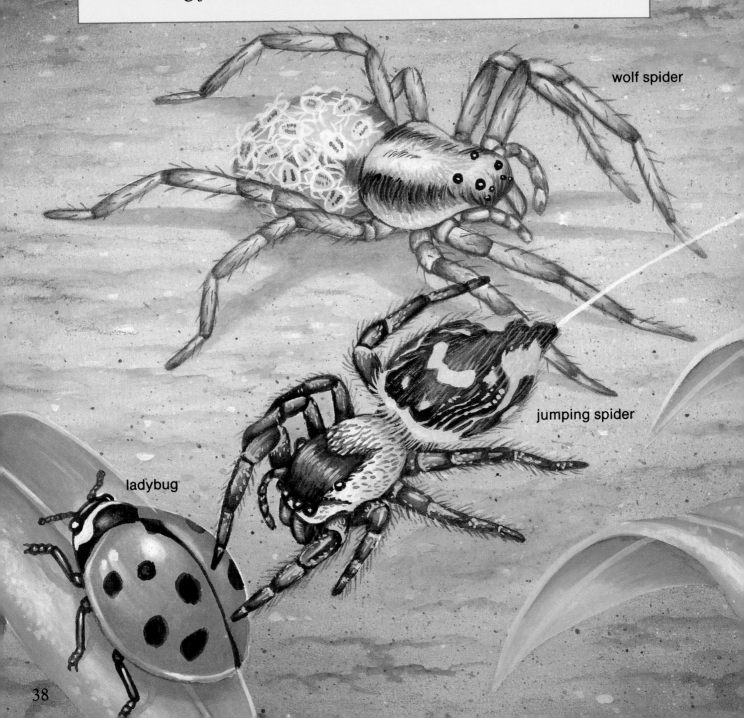

wolf spider

jumping spider

ladybug

Wolf spiders have a fine coat of short gray and brown hairs on their legs and bodies. You may see a wolf spider that seems to have a fuzzy gray covering on its back. Look closely and you will see dozens of baby spiders riding there. A female wolf spider carries its egg sac at the tip of its abdomen. When the spiderlings hatch, they climb onto their mother's back and ride for several days before setting off on their own.

Sometimes jumping spiders make a series of jumps as they chase an insect. Often a jumping spider makes one giant leap—as far as seven or eight inches—and clutches its prey with its powerful front legs. A jumping spider can leap many times its own length. Most jumping spiders are less than seven tenths of an inch long. Other spiders are as small as one twenty-fifth of an inch long as adults!

Look on and near the blossoms of flowers for crab spiders. Their long front legs are held open—crablike—ready to grab insects that are attracted to the flowers. Crab spiders also resemble crabs as they scuttle sideways or backward.

Although crab spiders are small, their poison acts quickly and kills much larger bees and butterflies. Their color helps make their ambushes successful. They are often yellow or white and match the petals or other flower parts where they crouch. Some crab spiders can change from white to yellow, or vice versa, when they move from one flower to another.

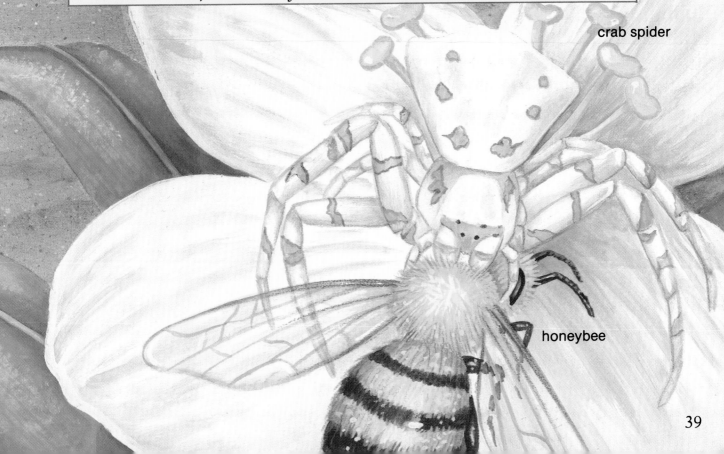

crab spider

honeybee

39

Mexican tarantula

The Biggest Spiders

The biggest spiders are called Hairy Mygalomorphs by scientists. Most people call them tarantulas. The largest kinds, from South America, measure ten inches across their bodies and legs. About 30 species live in the southwestern United States. Because of their size and shaggy look, tarantulas frighten people. But the tarantulas of the United States are not dangerous. The bite of an American tarantula may cause a slight swelling, or have no effect at all. Many species of tarantulas are easy to tame, and people keep them as pets. A female tarantula may live 20 years.

A jewelry store in New York City once used tarantulas as "guard spiders." Tarantulas and warning signs were put in window display cases at night. The spiders were a success, because most people believe they are dangerous.

scorpion

trapdoor spider

In the wild, tarantulas live in burrows that they dig with their jaws. They creep out to hunt at night. Trapdoor spiders, related to tarantulas, also dig burrows in the soil. They line their hideouts with silk.

Some trapdoor spiders make doors of mud mixed with silk. Other kinds make thin doors of silk alone. In either case the doors swing open and shut on hinges spun from silk. A spider waits inside its burrow, behind its door. It dashes out to grab a passing insect, then hurries home and shuts its door. Its burrow becomes a dining room.

Exploring the World of Insects and Spiders

A biologist named Frank Lutz once wrote a book called *A Lot of Insects*. It was about the insects that Lutz found on one small plot of land, his house lot in New Jersey. He identified more than 1,500 species.

Anyone who begins to look closely at grasses, weeds, flowers, and other plants will discover a surprising variety of insects and spiders. Although some species flee from people, others stay when approached. With a magnifying glass you may see a beetle's mouthparts or a spider's spinnerets in action. You may witness a dramatic battle between predator and prey.

Your curiosity may lead you to books that help identify the animals you see. Perhaps you will want to capture some insects or spiders to observe them more closely, then let them go.

While some people make collections of dried insect specimens, others simply enjoy watching the creatures that share our homes, backyards, and neighborhoods. Look for insects and spiders at different times of day, and in different kinds of weather. Find out what insects and spiders do when it rains. See how their behavior changes as the seasons change.

The world of insects and spiders invites you to explore.

Index